Feel Fearless Flapjacks

Look out for more

Bake a Wish

books:

Feel Good Fairy Cakes

Can-Do Crispies

Get-Better Jelly

Bake a Wish

Feel Fearless Flapjacks

Lorna Honeywell

Illustrated by Samantha Chaffey

SCHOLASTIC

With special thanks to Pearl Morrison

First published in the UK in 2012 by Scholastic Children's Books
An imprint of Scholastic Ltd
Euston House, 24 Eversholt Street
London, NW1 1DB, UK
Registered office: Westfield Road, Southam, Warwickshire, CV47 0RA
SCHOLASTIC and associated logos are trademarks
and/or registered trademarks of Scholastic Inc.

The right of Lorna Honeywell and Samantha Chaffey to be identified as the
author and illustrator of this work has been asserted by them.
Produced by Hothouse Fiction.
www.hothousefiction.com

ISBN 978 1 407 13116 0

A CIP catalogue record for this book is available
from the British Library.

Printed and bound by CPI Group (UK) Ltd, Croydon, CR0 4YY
Papers used by Scholastic Children's Books are made from
wood grown in sustainable forests.

1 3 5 7 9 10 8 6 4 2

www.scholastic.co.uk/zone

For Kitty Morrison,
also affectionately known as Granny Orkney.

And for Auriol Bussell,
the best grandma anyone could wish for.

Playing Pirates!

Lily Dalton wriggled and jiggled and squirmed in the front seat of the car.

"Sit still!" Mum told her again.

"I can't," Lily giggled. "I'm just too excited about seeing Izzy!"

Lily grinned as she thought about her cousin. Isabelle was coming to stay at Grandma and Grandpa's house, and Mum was taking Lily and

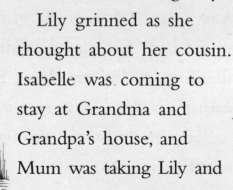

her little brother, Archie, round to play with her. Izzy and her family lived too far away to visit very often, but whenever they did Lily always had lots of fun with her.

The last time Izzy had visited they had pretended to have ponies called Peanut and Princess. All afternoon they'd galloped around Grandpa's garden, jumping over flowerpots and trotting around the grass. When they were too tired to run any more they'd used the garden shed as a stable.

They had so much fun together that sometimes they even pretended that they were sisters, not cousins. *It would be fun to have a sister*, Lily thought, glancing at Archie in the back seat, playing with one of his toy dinosaurs. Archie gave her a big smile. *But having a brother is quite good too!* Lily smiled.

"How long is Izzy staying?" Archie asked their mum.

"For the whole weekend," Mum smiled. "While Auntie Helen and Uncle Mike go on a little holiday."

Lily gave a big disappointed sigh. "I wish she could stay for ever."

As the car pulled up outside Grandma and Grandpa's house, Lily could see Grandpa cutting the hedge in the front garden.

He waved and Lily jumped out to give him a hug before dashing inside. She and Archie didn't usually go to Grandma and Grandpa's at the weekend because they stayed with them every day after school until Mum and Dad finished work. But today was special. Izzy would be there!

"Hi, Grandpa!" Archie yelled as he sped past him, trying to overtake Lily as she ran, panting, into the hall. She kicked off her shoes and dashed into the kitchen.

Grandma was singing along to the radio as she did some washing up. The sleeves on her bright green jumper were rolled up to her elbows and her hands were all bubbly with soap suds. Hector, her marmalade-coloured cat, was snoozing on the window sill.

"Goodness," Grandma said, as Lily stood in the doorway gasping for breath.

"Hello, you two. You're in a hurry!"

Lily looked around the kitchen.
"Where's Izzy?" she panted.

"Oh, she's not here yet." Grandma told
her. "The traffic must be bad."

Lily let her little rucksack drop to the
floor and groaned with disappointment.

"I'm sure she'll be here very soon,"
Grandma smiled. She dried her hands and

switched off the radio. "Why don't you and Archie help me get the yellow room ready while we're waiting?"

Archie screwed up his face. "That's not much fun."

"I'm sure we can find a way to make it fun," Grandma smiled. "Let's go up there and see."

Lily and Archie charged into the hall and raced upstairs. This time Archie won and he threw open the door to Grandma's spare bedroom. It was called the yellow room because it had yellow curtains, and the wallpaper was covered with tiny yellow flowers. There was a window seat, too, that looked out over the front garden. Lily could see Grandpa down there busily working in the garden.

While Grandma opened the bottom

drawer of the wardrobe and took out sheets, pillowcases and a duvet cover, Lily and Archie scrambled to sit on the bouncy double bed. Hector jumped up next to them and lay on Lily's lap.

"Now." Grandma shook the big white sheet out high above their heads, again and again. "What does this look like?" she asked. Lily stared at the sheet as it rippled like the sail of a tall ship blowing and flapping in an imaginary wind.

"A sail," Lily guessed.

"Oh yes." Grandma agreed. "And that must make you ... pirates!"

"Aaarrrr!" Archie yelled.

"Yes, Captain Grandma!" Lily squealed with delight as Grandma let the sheet float down on top of her and Archie. They giggled and wriggled, getting more and more tangled up in the bedding.

"This won't get the ship ready for Pirate Izzy," Grandma said eventually. "All hands on deck, sailors."

While Lily helped Grandma tuck the sheet in at all four corners of the mattress, Archie scrambled off the bed and ran over to the window. "I'm going to watch for more pirate ships." He climbed up on the window seat and held his hands up to his eye to make a telescope.

"Any ships ahoy?" Grandma asked Archie.

Archie swung his telescope up and down the road. "Yes!" he suddenly called out. "Not a ship though, a car — they're here!" Just then they heard the cheerful beep-beep of a car horn.

Lily rushed to the window. She could see Grandpa waving to a blue car as it parked outside the gate.

"It's Izzy!" Lily squealed, and she
turned and ran downstairs, followed by
Archie, Grandma and Hector. Lily pulled
open the front door just as Auntie Helen
and Uncle Mike were getting out of the
car.

"Hello," they called as Lily rushed
down the garden path. Auntie Helen was
getting some things out of the boot and
Uncle Mike was talking to Grandpa about

the traffic. But where was Izzy?

Lily hopped from one foot to the other impatiently. And then at last Izzy appeared at the garden gate. She was clutching a soft toy so tightly in front of her face that all Lily could see was her blonde hair and two red hair clasps.

Lily waved excitedly with both hands and gave an extra-happy smile. But Izzy didn't wave, and she kept her face buried in her toy.

That's funny, Lily thought. She tried

again. "Hi, Izzy!" she called. Izzy glanced up and Lily saw why she had been hiding her face. Little wet silvery streaks were running down her cheeks – Izzy was crying!

2

What's Wrong, Izzy?

Grandma walked down the path towards Izzy with her arms open. "It's so nice to see you," she said, giving Izzy a hug. She looked at the soft toy Izzy was clutching. "And you've brought Piggy to stay, too."

"I don't want to stay!" Izzy sniffed. She held Piggy tighter and stared at the ground. "I want to go home! I want to sleep in my own room."

"But I have so many nice things planned for us to do," Grandma replied, crouching down so that she was Izzy's height.

"It's only for two sleeps," Uncle Mike said. "You'll have a lovely time."

"And Lily and Archie have come over to play especially," Grandma told her. "They've been looking forward to seeing you."

Izzy peered out from behind Piggy and looked at Lily and Archie. Lily smiled and nodded.

"Everyone's so pleased that you've come to visit," Grandpa said.

Hector jumped down from the gate and wrapped his tail around Izzy's legs, purring loudly.

"Even Hector!" Lily added.

Izzy gave a sniffly smile and Grandpa took a clean handkerchief from his pocket and gently wiped the tears from her eyes.

Auntie Helen handed a pink bag to Grandma. "Izzy's pyjamas are in there, and

a few other things, too," she said, giving
Grandma a kiss on the cheek. Then she
bent down to give Izzy a big hug. "We
need to leave now," she said, kissing the
top of Izzy's head. "But we'll phone you
in the morning. OK?"

Izzy looked as if she might start
crying again, so Lily held her hand as
they waved goodbye to Uncle Mike and
Auntie Helen's car.

"What are we going to do now?" Lily asked as the car drove out of sight. She was worried Izzy would ask to go home again.

"Well," Grandma said, "We could go to the swings, or we could feed the ducks, or..."

"Build a den!" Archie said, hopefully.

Grandma laughed. "Maybe ... but let's take Izzy's bag into the house and have a drink before we decide."

While Grandma and Archie walked inside, Lily looked down at her little cousin. "I'll be your big sister today," Lily told her reassuringly. "Do you want to tell me what's wrong? Don't you like coming to visit Grandma and Grandpa?"

Izzy sniffed. "Yes, but not to sleep."

"But you've got Piggy to keep you company." Lily touched his little pink ears.

Izzy stroked the toy pig's snout. "Piggy doesn't want to stay either!"

Lily wondered what she could do to make Izzy happy. It would need to be something very special indeed. She thought and she thought and she thought. Then she had an idea – there was one thing she knew would *definitely* stop Izzy feeling sad.

Lily squeezed Izzy's hand. "Don't worry," she told Izzy. "I know just the thing to cheer you up!"

Lily led her little cousin inside. In the kitchen Grandma was putting the kettle on for a cup of tea. While it boiled she poured juice into three coloured cups.

"So," Grandma asked as she sat down at the table and gently lifted Izzy on to her knee. "Are you going to tell us why you don't want to stay over?"

Izzy just shrugged her shoulders and

hugged Piggy tighter.

"Have a drink of juice?" Archie
suggested. "That'll cheer you up!"

"Juice isn't going to make Izzy happy," Lily told him. "But I've got an idea that will..." She grinned at Archie.

Archie bounced up and down. "You mean our special secret?"

"Yes!" Lily clapped her hands in excitement.

"What a good idea!" Grandma smiled.

Izzy was staring at them all. "What secret?" she asked curiously.

"We know magic!" Lily squealed.

Izzy looked confused. "*Real* magic?"

Lily nodded. She couldn't stop smiling. "Real magic that will definitely help you feel better!"

As Grandma stretched her arms up towards a yellow stripy jar on the top shelf of the dresser, Lily explained.

* * * 17

"Grandma's got a *magic* jar," she told Izzy, smiling at her cousin's amazed face. "Whenever there's a problem, ingredients and a magic recipe appear in it, and it tells us something wonderful to bake to make things better!"

"Really?" Izzy gasped, looking at the jar in amazement.

"Really!" Lily grinned. "When I was too nervous to sing in the school Easter show, we made Can-Do Crispies!" She smiled proudly. "I sang louder than anyone else. And when Archie was in a bad mood we made Feel Good Fairy Cakes! And guess what...?"

"I was happy straight away," Archie answered. "*And* Get-Better Jelly helped me when I was poorly."

"I had a sore throat last week," Izzy told him. "But I had to have medicine."

"The recipes are sort of like a magical medicine," Lily explained, "because they always make us feel better when something's wrong. Don't they, Grandma?"

"They certainly do," Grandma agreed.

Izzy had a little think. "Will the jar have a recipe to stop me being scared of the dark?"

"Ah!" said Grandma. She looked at Izzy kindly "So *that's* why you're unhappy about staying over."

Izzy gave a shy nod and hugged Piggy.

Grandma smiled. "In that case, the jar can *definitely* help you."

Izzy stared at the stripy jar. "How does it work?"

"You have to put your fingers on the jar and close your eyes. Then make a wish," Lily told her. She closed her eyes to show Izzy what to do. "Tell the jar you don't want to be scared of the dark. When you open it, the magical recipe will be inside!"

"Wow!" Izzy grinned. "And it will really work?"

"Yes!" Lily nodded. Izzy reached out to gently touch the jar with her fingertips and closed her eyes. "I wish I wasn't scared of the dark," she whispered.

She opened her eyes and a little smile
appeared at the corner of her mouth.
"Can I see the magic now?" she asked.

3

Baking a Wish

Izzy put Piggy down on the table and climbed up on a chair. She put one arm around the jar to hold it steady and lifted the lid.

"What can you see?" Archie asked.

Izzy peered into the jar. "Hmmm," she said and pulled out a bag of porridge oats. "That's not very magical." She put her hand back inside the jar and brought out a bag of raisins. She looked puzzled. "It's just like breakfast,"

she said,
and set the
bag down
next to the
porridge
oats.

"Is there
anything
else?" Lily
asked.

Izzy put
her hand back inside the jar and wriggled
it around. This time she pulled out a
piece of paper.

"That's the magic recipe!" Lily
squealed and she gave a little excited
bounce.

Izzy handed the recipe to Grandma.
"But it's just instructions. How do we
know what it makes?"

"Grandma always knows," Lily said proudly.

Grandma looked at the recipe carefully. "Very interesting ... very interesting... *This* recipe," Grandma announced in a very grand voice, "is for *Feel Fearless Flapjacks!*" She looked at Izzy with twinkling eyes. "Once you've eaten a Feel Fearless Flapjack, you won't be afraid of anything!"

"Really?" A smile spread across Izzy's face. "Can we bake my wish now?"

Grandma's eyes twinkled. "Oh yes. The sooner we start baking, the sooner you won't be afraid of the dark."

"We always wash our hands before baking," Lily told Izzy. Archie had already dashed over to the sink. He was squeezing liquid soap out of the bottle on to his hands.

"Grandma's soap is really, really bubbly,"

he told Izzy. He turned on the tap
and let the water run over his fingers.
"Watch!" he said and squeezed his hands
into tight fists. Tiny bubbles floated up
between his fingers.

Izzy squealed with delight. "Let me try."

Soon, bubbles were floating all over the
sink.

Once their hands were squeaky clean,
it was time to put on their aprons.
Archie wore his dinosaur apron. When
Lily put on her apron, Izzy squealed, "It's
got cupcake pockets!" She looked up at
Grandma. "Which one can I wear?"

"You can borrow one of mine,"
Grandma said.

Izzy chose the apron with a teapot
pattern all over it. It was much too long
but Grandma rolled it up at the waist and
tied a big bow at the front to hold it in

place. "Now we're ready to start baking!" she said.

Grandma picked up the recipe from the table. "We've already got the porridge oats and raisins." She pointed to the butter dish on the table. "And we've got a whole block of butter, too. All we need now is golden syrup and brown sugar."

"I'll get them!" Lily cried. "Follow me, Izzy! I know where they're kept!"

She couldn't wait to show Izzy the Yummy Cupboard, where Grandma stored all her baking ingredients. She pulled the door open and Izzy followed her inside.

"It's like a little shop," Izzy said as she gazed up at all the shelves full of packets and bottles and bags and jars. "And it smells of jelly beans and popcorn."

"My favourite!" said Archie, who had squeezed inside the cupboard with them.

Lily reached up to the shelf where Grandma kept the tin of syrup and handed it to Izzy. She found the bag of brown sugar and gave it to Archie, and then she took one last look around the shelves. "See you soon," she told the cupboard before going out and closing the door.

Lily, Archie and Izzy laughed as they raced back over to the kitchen table. Grandma had got a pan out from the cupboard and now she was setting the scales down on the table.

"The first thing we need to do is measure out the butter," she said. "We're going to need one hundred and twenty-five grams. That's exactly half a block of butter." She started to cut it into little chunks. "I'll chop it up into smaller pieces so it will melt easier," she explained.

"Then all the butter pieces go into the pan. Do you want to help, Archie?"

Grandma gave Archie a wooden spoon and tilted the dish so he could chase the slippery butter cubes into the pan.

"This is fun," he said.

"What can we do?" Lily asked.

"Hmmm, why don't you and Izzy weigh the sugar?" Grandma suggested.

"Oh yes!" Lily smiled.

Izzy carefully poured the sugar on to the scales a little at a time. Lily watched

the little hand on the dial move round as the dish grew heavier and heavier. "We need fifty-five grams," Lily told her. "I'll tell you when to stop pouring."

Izzy looked at Lily and smiled as the sugar spilled on to the scales. "I like having you for my sister," she grinned.

4

Flapjacks, not Flatjacks!

Everyone in the kitchen was very busy. Even Hector was busy watching the sugar pouring out. Every time he moved his head the little bell on his collar started ringing.

Archie wiped his hands on his apron. "All the butter is in the pan, Grandma."

"Then the next thing we need to do is melt it," Grandma said.

She carried the pan over to the hob. "The butter must be melted very gently so it doesn't burn," she told Archie.

"Stop!" Lily said. "We've got enough sugar, Izzy!"

"Well done," Grandma told them. "We'll add the sugar to the butter when Archie's finished."

Lily and Izzy came over to watch as Archie pulled a chair over to the hob and climbed up on it. Grandma held the pan steady while Archie gently stirred the soft butter with a wooden spoon. Round and round went the knobs of butter, slowly spreading out across the bottom of the pan as they dissolved, turning from pale yellow to a clear golden liquid. "It's just like melting chocolate," he said, "except it doesn't smell as yummy."

"I think that's done," Grandma said.

She helped Archie jump down from the
chair before carrying the pan of melted
butter over to the table and putting it on
a wooden chopping board.

"Can I put the sugar in?" Izzy asked.

"Careful, the pan will be hot," Grandma

warned as she set it down. She used her oven gloves to hold the pan still while Izzy slowly poured the sugar into the melted butter.

Lily started reading the recipe. "Next we need to add the syrup."

Archie picked up the syrup tin. "It looks just like a paint pot!"

"Remember, syrup is very runny and very sticky," Grandma told him as she put a spoon under the edge of the lid and popped it open. Archie, Lily and Izzy peered inside at the thick shiny liquid. "That means it can be very messy."

"I'll be *extra* very careful," Archie promised.

Grandma opened the lid and handed Archie a tablespoon. He dipped the spoon into the golden syrup and twirled it around. "How many spoonfuls do we need?"

"We need three," Grandma told him.

Archie climbed up on the chair to reach the pan and drizzled the syrup into it, swishing the spoon around until every last gloopy drop slid off the spoon.

"Good job," Grandma praised him as she put the pan back on the hob. "Now we need to mix everything together. I'll do the stirring," she said. "But I've got a very important job for you three. We need to make sure that the mixture goes nice and bubbly – so you have to be on bubble watch. Make sure you tell me if you see one!"

Lily stared at the pan. The sugar scraped against the bottom of the pan as it slowly melted into the butter and syrup. Grandma's spoon went round and round and soon a warm, sweet smell started to fill the kitchen. Hector's nose twitched.

Suddenly Lily spotted a bubble rising up through the syrup and popping on the surface. "Saw one!" she smiled.

"There's another one!" Izzy grinned.

"I want to see one!" Archie complained.

"Just watch, Archie, soon there'll be lots and lots." Grandma told him. She was right. Bubble after bubble popped inside the pot.

Izzy's eyes grew wide as she stared at the mixture. "It's bubblier than your soap, Grandma!"

Grandma smiled. "Well, that means it's ready! It's time to add the oats."

Grandma carried the hot pan back over to the table and set it down on the chopping board. She used her oven gloves to hold it steady while Lily sprinkled the oats into the pan.

"This time you can stir," Grandma told her. "Make sure the oats are completely covered with the mixture."

"It smells really nice," Izzy said. "I didn't know you could cook magic."

"It's just like mixing a potion," Archie told her. "You stir everything together and then magic happens."

"And we're not finished making our magic potion yet," Grandma said. "Izzy?

Will you add the raisins, please?"

Izzy opened the bag and poured them
in to the mixture. While she stirred,
Izzy asked, "What are raisins made from,
Grandma?"

"Raisins are dried grapes," Grandma
told her.

Izzy peered into the pan. "They don't
look like grapes."

"That's because all the juice has
been squeezed out of them," Grandma
explained. "Like
they've had a really,
really tight hug!"
Grandma picked up
Archie and gave
him a squeeze.

"Stop!" he
laughed. "I don't
want to be a raisin!"

Lily handed Izzy a raisin and she popped it in her mouth. "Mmm," she said. "They're sweet and chewy."

It was Archie's turn to stir. "It smells so yummy," he said. "I wish I could eat it now!"

"It's almost ready," Grandma said, pulling a baking tin out of the cupboard.

"Can I pour the mixture into the tin, Grandma?" Lily asked.

"There's something very important we need to do first," Grandma told her. She tore away two pieces of the butter wrapping and handed one to Lily and one to Izzy.

Izzy screwed up her nose. "What's this for?"

"To grease the tin," Grandma said. "Rub the pan with the buttery paper and it will get nice and slippery. Then the flapjacks won't stick to it when they're cooked."

"That's a good idea," Izzy said as she and Lily started sliding the butter all over the tin.

When the tin was all buttery, Grandma lifted the pan up and tilted it over the tin while Lily, Izzy and Archie scooped out the mixture with their wooden spoons. The flapjack mixture dropped into the tin in gooey lumps.

"Make sure to scrape it all out," Grandma said.

"That's because we want every little bit of magic!" Lily told Izzy.

"Now pat the mixture down in the tin with the back of the spoon," Grandma said. "Make sure it's all stuck together."

They patted and patted until Archie got carried away and started hitting the mixture so hard with his spoon that Grandma had to tell him to stop. "We want flapjacks," she reminded him, "not *flat*jacks!"

Lily and Izzy giggled.

The flapjacks were now ready to be cooked. "Stand back!" Grandma said as she opened the oven door. Hot air blasted out into the kitchen. "That's as hot as a volcano," Archie said.

"Who wants to set the timer?"
Grandma asked as she shut the oven door.

"Me!" Izzy shouted happily. Lily smiled.
Izzy seemed to have forgotten all about
being frightened of the dark. The Feel
Fearless Flapjacks were working already!

5

A Slippery Surprise!

Lily helped Izzy set the tomato-shaped timer so that it would ring after twenty minutes. "Then we'll know the flapjacks are ready," she told Izzy. "We don't want them to burn."

There was one last thing to do. Lily took a pen and in her neatest writing wrote "Feel Fearless Flapjacks" on the top of the recipe. She then took it over to her special recipe box on the dresser and popped it inside. "There!" she said happily.

But then she
stopped.
She'd like
to be able
to make
Feel Fearless
Flapjacks
whenever she
wanted to —
but there was
someone else who needed the magical
recipe more than she did.

Lily glanced over at her little cousin,
then pulled the recipe out of the box.
"You should have this, Izzy," she said,
offering it to her.

"Oh! That's *very* nice of you, Lily," said
Grandma. "But I've got an even better
idea — why don't I copy it out so that
you can *both* have the recipe?"

"Yes, please!" Lily cried, feeling relieved. She was so pleased that she could keep the recipe after all – and that Izzy would have it too.

"While the flapjacks are cooking and I'm writing the recipe, why don't you two go upstairs to the yellow room and help Izzy unpack her overnight things?" Grandma suggested.

"I've brought my jewellery box, and all my rings and necklaces," Lily told Izzy. "Do you want to see them?"

Izzy nodded excitedly. But Archie scowled.

"That's girl stuff," he said and pulled off his apron. "I'm going out to the garden to look for slugs."

Archie pulled on his wellingtons and marched outside.

Lily slung her little rucksack over her

shoulder then picked up Izzy's bag. "I'll carry it upstairs for you."

Izzy's bag was very full. Lily wondered what was inside it – it seemed like her little cousin had packed enough things to stay for a week!

Lily didn't have to wonder for long, because as soon as they got to the yellow room Izzy opened her bag and started pulling things out. Inside were her pyjamas, toothbrush and clean clothes, but there was also a floppy teddy, a green frog, a pink kitten and a brown velvet dog that barked when you pulled a string on its tummy.

Izzy climbed up on the big double bed and started to plan where her soft toys were going to sleep that night. "Piggy always sleeps next to me," she told Lily.

Lily opened her own rucksack and brought out her bright red jewellery box.

Izzy's eyes widened when she saw all Lily's rings and bracelets and necklaces.

"You can try on any of them you like," Lily told her.

"This is my favourite," Izzy said, slipping a red glittery butterfly bracelet on to her wrist. The sun was shining into the room, making the jewellery extra sparkly. They sat cross-legged on the big comfy yellow duvet, decorating each other with necklaces and rings.

"We look like princesses sitting on a big yellow sunflower," Izzy giggled.

"See!" said Lily. "It's not scary in this room, is it?"

"No," Izzy said. "But that's because you're here." Her voice started to shake and her bottom lip quivered. "When you go home I'll be all alone in the dark."

"You won't be scared of the dark after you've eaten a flapjack," Lily reminded her. "You'll feel fearless!"

"But how can a flapjack stop me being scared?" Izzy asked anxiously.

"Because they're magic." Lily laughed. "You'll see!"

"That's right," Grandma said from the doorway. A lovely smell of warm flapjacks was drifting up from the kitchen. "The flapjacks will certainly stop you being scared," Grandma continued, "but there's no

reason why Lily can't stay over tonight as
well. There's plenty of room for you both."

Lily looked at Izzy. "A sleepover!" she
cried.

"Yay!" Izzy yelled, bouncing up and
down on the bed. "Thank you, Grandma.
Thank you, thank you!"

Her necklaces and bracelets jangled and swung around as she jumped up and down.

"It's going to be such fun!" Izzy said with an extra-high bounce.

"We can have a midnight feast!" Lily squealed.

Izzy stopped bouncing. She was looking worried again. "It's very dark at midnight."

"But I'll be with you!" Lily said, taking Izzy by the hand and bouncing again. They carried on bouncing and giggling so much that Grandma started chuckling too. But as they laughed, a terrified shriek came from downstairs.

Lily gasped. "That was Archie! Something's happened to him!"

Grandma ran out of the room, faster than Lily had ever seen her move before. Lily leapt from the bed, landed on the floor with a thud and rushed after her, followed by Izzy, who was tightly clutching Piggy.

Downstairs, Archie was screaming. "Snake!" he yelled. "Snake!"

6

Snake Search

Archie was in the kitchen, leaning heavily against the back door. He was breathing very quickly and pointing towards the garden. "There's a snake out there!" he gasped. "A poisonous one!"

Grandma rushed over to check that he was OK. She scooped him up and kissed the top of his head.

"It was scary," Archie told her.

"You scared *me*!" Grandma squeezed him tight. "I thought you'd hurt yourself!"

She walked over to the window and she and Archie looked out. "Now, are you sure it was a snake? Where did you see it?"

"Yes!" Archie insisted. He looked up at Lily. His eyes were wide and staring. "It was eeenormous!"

Everyone jumped as the back door opened. Archie gave a yell and leaped up on a chair in a panic.

"Shut the door! Shut the door!" he shouted as Grandpa walked into the kitchen.

Grandpa quickly closed it. "What's wrong?" he asked. "I've never seen you run so fast, Archie!"

"SNAKE!" they all shouted.

"Where?" Grandpa asked, looking around the kitchen.

"In the garden!" Archie told him.

"Under the strawberry bushes. Didn't you see it?"

"No, I just saw you racing inside!" Grandpa said. "I'm glad you're all right."

"Archie said it was huge and poisonous," Izzy told him.

Lily pushed against the closed door to make sure it was tightly shut. "Don't worry," she told her. "The snake can't get in now."

"I don't like snakes," Izzy said. She stared at the door, as if she was looking for gaps a snake could slither under.

Lily reached out and grabbed Izzy's hand.

"You don't need to be scared," Grandpa told Archie. "Most snakes in this country are harmless. They're *much* more scared of us than we are of them. But I should probably go and check that the chickens are OK."

He looked at them all, one by one. "Anyone want to come with me?"

Lily looked at Archie and Izzy. Archie was shaking his head so fast that he was almost a blur. "I don't think so, Grandpa," Lily told him.

Grandma looked down at Lily, Izzy and Archie and smiled. "Well, it's a good thing we made Feel Fearless Flapjacks." She pointed to the table. "And it's a very good thing that they are ready to eat."

Lily had been so worried about Archie and the enormous poisonous snake that she hadn't noticed the kitchen was filled with a delicious smell. The tray of flapjacks was cooling on the kitchen table.

The snake was forgotten as everyone dashed over to the table to watch Grandma cut the flapjacks into little squares.

"They look so yummy," Archie said, leaning over the table.

Grandma started putting the flapjack pieces on to plates. "Would anyone like a glass of milk?" she asked.

Three hands shot up. "Yes, please!"

Everyone sat up at the kitchen table and Grandma passed round the plates. Lily licked her lips as she slid into a seat next to Archie.

Her brother was crouched on his chair with his feet tucked under his legs. "Why are you sitting like that?" she asked.

"In case a snake slithers by," he said before taking a bite of flapjack.

Lily picked her flapjack up and nibbled it. It was sweet and juicy and crumbly and delicious!

"Flapjacks don't taste like cereal," Archie mumbled. His mouth was very full.

"They taste a bit like cake and a bit like a biscuit," Lily decided. "The raisins are really chewy."

Izzy rubbed
her stomach. "I
like the way
they make my
tummy feel
warm inside."

"That'll be
the magic,"
Archie said.
"Are you still
scared of the dark?"

"Well, I won't know until night-time,"
Izzy shrugged.

"Hmmmm, that's a long time to wait,"
Lily thought out loud.

Archie swallowed the last mouthful
of his flapjack. "I know how to test the
magic right now." He climbed down from
the chair. "I'll go out into the garden
with Grandpa. If I'm not scared of the

snake, that means the magic has worked!"

"That's a good idea," Lily told him.

"Yes," Izzy agreed. "If the magic fixed Archie then it'll have worked for me too." Izzy popped the last bit of her flapjack in her mouth and climbed down from her chair.

Lily stood up and brushed crumbs from her fingers. "We'll come with you, Archie," she said bravely. "We'll search for the snake together!"

Fearless Archie!

Grandma, Lily and Izzy quickly pulled on their shoes. Grandpa and Archie were still wearing their wellies. Grandpa opened the door and led the way outside. "Now, where did you see this enormous snake?"

"Over there," Archie said pointing to the strawberry bush. "Next to the chicken coop."

"Follow me," Grandpa said. He took slow, quiet steps towards the strawberry bushes, just like Hector when he was getting ready to pounce.

Izzy clutched Lily's hand. "Do you think the snake's as big as me?"

"Bigger!" Archie called back over his shoulder as he set off to follow Grandpa.

"Don't worry," Lily told her, trying to sound brave. "I'll protect you." But they stood a little way back, behind Grandma, just in case.

Grandma's chickens, Bessie and Jessie, flapped up to the fence around their coop and started clucking. They looked very curious about what was happening. Their heads darted back and forth as they watched Grandpa and Archie walk slowly by. Bessie spread her wings and clucked again when Grandpa crouched down on the ground and looked under the strawberry bush.

Izzy tightened her grip on Lily's hand.
"I hope the snake doesn't bite Grandpa."

"It won't," Grandma promised her. Lily
crossed her fingers.

"Can you see it yet, Grandpa?" Archie
whispered.

"Aha!" Grandpa said and suddenly slid
his arm under the bush.

Archie took a nervous step backwards

as Grandpa stood up. In his hand was the snake. "Got it!"

"We caught the snake!" Archie called out.

"It doesn't look very big," Izzy whispered.

"Oh! Isn't it pretty!" Grandma said, going over to see it.

Lily took a step forward to get a closer look. The snake was brown and had black stripes running along its sides that rippled as it curled round Grandpa's fingers.

"It's not much longer than one of my necklaces," she smiled.

"That's because it's not a snake," Grandpa told them. "It's called a slow worm and it's actually a lizard, like a gecko or an iguana."

"It *looks* like a snake," Archie said hesitantly. "It doesn't even have any legs!" he added.

"It's a bit of a funny name, because it's not really a worm either," Grandpa explained. "But it is a lizard. Snakes don't have eyelids. And it can make its tail fall off if it gets trapped. Snakes can't do that."

"Cooooool," Archie grinned.

Grandpa was holding the slow worm just behind its head. His other hand gently held the end of its body to stop it from wriggling. "But we're not going to make its tail drop off because it takes a long time for it to grow back again." He held it out towards Archie. "Do you want to touch it?" he asked. Archie shook his head nervously.

"Remember, he's much more frightened of you than you are of him," Grandma reminded Archie. "You look like a giant to a slow worm."

"We should feed it a Feel Fearless Flapjack!" Lily giggled.

But Izzy wasn't laughing. "The magic didn't work!" she gasped. "Archie's still scared!"

Archie glared at her. "No I'm not!" He reached out and gently stroked its back. "See. I'm not afraid."

"Me either!" Lily said. "I like the slow worm," she added as she reached out and touched his smooth back.

Izzy shyly held out her hand as well and gave the slow worm a tiny stroke. "It's not slimy!" she said.

"No, he's got lovely scales," Grandpa told her. He stroked it again.

"Can I keep it as a pet?" Archie asked.

"I think we should let him go now," Grandpa said. "Leave him to carry on hunting for snails and slugs to eat."

"Yuck!" said Izzy.

"To a slow worm, snails and slugs are as delicious as flapjacks!" Grandma told her.

"Can I set it free?" Archie asked. He carefully took the slow worm out of Grandpa's hands and gently put it down on the ground under the strawberry bush. As it slithered away he said, "Snakes aren't scary at all now I'm fearless."

Lily grinned as her little brother raced off, pretending to be Superman. She hoped the flapjacks would make Izzy fearless as well!

A Midnight Feast

Later that night, Lily and Izzy were in the bathroom brushing their teeth. Mum had dropped off Lily's overnight things when she came to take Archie home, and Lily was wearing her favourite pyjamas, the ones with pink stripes. Izzy's had purple flowers on them. Hector was curled up on the bath mat listening to them chat.

"I like feeling brave," Izzy said through a mouth full of toothpaste.

"And if you ever feel scared again, all

you have to do is make Feel Fearless
Flapjacks!" Lily told her.

Grandma peered round the bathroom door. "Bedtime!" she smiled.

Lily and Izzy rinsed their toothbrushes and ran through to the yellow room. Hector followed with his collar bell ringing. The girls jumped into the big double bed and Izzy arranged all her toys.

There were so many that there wasn't much room for Lily! She wriggled until she was comfy, then snuggled down under the covers.

"Can you sing us the lullaby song, Grandma?" Lily asked.

Grandma finished tucking them in and sat down on the edge of the bed.

"Roses whisper, goodnight," Grandma sang in her soft voice, "in the silvery light..."

Lily loved the goodnight song Grandma always sang whenever she and Archie stayed overnight. She yawned, but she wouldn't close her eyes yet, not until she knew Izzy was OK.

Grandma's lullaby made Lily feel sleepy, warm and cosy. Grandma finished her song and whispered, "Are you happy for me to turn off the light?"

Lily looked at Izzy. She nodded. "I'm not scared of the dark any more."

Grandma kissed them goodnight and switched off the bedside lamp. "Sleep tight," she whispered as she and Hector tiptoed out of the room and closed the door behind them.

The room was suddenly very quiet and very black. It took a moment for Lily's eyes to get used to the darkness. She could see the faint orange glow of a street light beyond the curtain and the shadowy shapes of the wardrobe and the chest of drawers.

"Are you OK, Izzy?" Lily whispered. "Can you see anything?"

"No," came Izzy's muffled voice from under the duvet. "I've got my eyes shut."

"Open your eyes and count to ten," Lily told her. "By the time you get to number nine, your eyes will be able to see in the dark."

"One … two … three…" Lily heard Izzy whisper. "Ten!" she said finally. "I can see you — and it's not scary at all! I can see the chair and the picture on the wall and…" There was a small, loud explosion from downstairs. Izzy dived back under the covers. "What was that?" she squealed.

Lily giggled. "It's only Grandpa sneezing."

Izzy peered out from under the duvet. They could hear Grandpa's feet climbing the stairs. He sneezed again before closing his bedroom door.

"Everyone's gone to bed," Lily whispered.

"It must be very, very late," Izzy said. "And I'm not sleepy any more!"

"Neither am I," Lily whispered. "I think I could stay awake all night."

"Me, too," Izzy agreed. She stared around the room. "Will it get any darker?"

"I don't think so," Lily told her.

"What if I wake up before morning and it's too dark to even see you?"

"Let's have a midnight feast of Feel Fearless Flapjacks," Lily told her. "Then you won't be afraid even if you do wake up."

"That's a good idea," Izzy said. "Is it midnight now?"

Lily wasn't sure, exactly, but she thought so. "It must be," she told Izzy. "We've been in bed for ages!"

She listened for any sound of Grandma and Grandpa, but the house was completely quiet. "Let's go," she whispered to Izzy. She pushed the duvet aside and climbed out of bed. "Remember to be very quiet," she reminded Izzy. "Walk on your tiptoes."

"I'm taking Piggy with me," Izzy whispered.

Lily opened the bedroom door and peered along the corridor. Moonlight was shining in through the hall window. They tiptoed past Grandma and Grandpa's room, then hurried downstairs.

The house was so silent all they could hear were their feet padding on the carpet and the ticking of the old clock in the sitting room.

They had reached the bottom step when Izzy grabbed the back of Lily's pyjama top. "Look!" she whispered. "Someone's there."

Lily gasped. A tall dark shape wearing a big hat was standing against the wall. Lily was about to turn and run back upstairs

when she realized the person wasn't moving. She took a closer look – and grinned in relief.

"It's OK. It's just the coat stand," she told Izzy. "Come on!" They crept on towards the kitchen and ran the last few steps. Lily opened the kitchen door and this time she was the one to jump. "Something just touched my leg!" she told Izzy. She could hear a soft growl, too.

"What is it?" Izzy squealed.

Lily looked down at a pair of green eyes staring back up at her. "Phew! It's only Hector."

Hector was so pleased to see them that he purred extra loudly. "Shhh!" Izzy giggled.

The kitchen was still warm even though it was night-time. It was dark, too, but Lily could see the flapjack tin on the kitchen table. She could just make out the red flowery pattern on it, although it looked grey in the darkness. Lily opened it as quietly as she could, and a lovely sweet flapjack smell burst into the kitchen.

"Yummy," Izzy whispered.

Lily had just handed Izzy a flapjack and taken one for herself when the kitchen light was suddenly switched on. Lily blinked in the bright glare. Grandpa was standing in the doorway in his pyjamas, holding a golf club as though he was about to throw it.

"Grandpa? Why aren't you asleep?" Lily asked.

Grandpa made a sound that was a bit like a laugh and a bit like a cough. He also went from looking very worried to looking very relieved.

"I heard a noise," he said. "I thought you were burglars!" He rested the golf club against the wall. "What are you two doing in here?" he asked.

"We're having a midnight feast of Feel Fearless Flapjacks," Lily told him.

"Just in case I wake up in the night and get scared," Izzy explained.

"And what is there to be scared of?" Grandpa asked.

"The dark," Izzy said. "I don't like the dark. Neither does Piggy."

"There's no need to be afraid of the dark," Grandpa told her.

Izzy pointed to the window. "But there might be scary monsters out there!"

Grandpa unlocked the back door. "Come and see," he said.

Izzy and Lily got up from the table and stood on the doorstep, looking out over the garden with Grandpa. The moon was very bright and the moonbeams made the grass and the rooftops silvery and sparkly, just like Lily's jewellery. Lily gasped at how beautiful it was. "It's magical," she whispered.

"No monsters," Grandpa told them. "Just Bessie and Jessie asleep in the coop." He pointed to the sky. "And a lovely smiley moon to watch over you and lots of stars to keep you company. They need the dark so they can sparkle so brightly."

Lily stared up at the sky in wonder.

"I like night-time," Izzy whispered. She hugged Piggy and gave a long, tired yawn.

Lily yawned too as she peered out into the shadows. "I wonder where the slow worm is?"

"Asleep," Grandpa said. "And you should be too." He ushered them inside

and closed the door.

They *were* very sleepy. Izzy was too sleepy to even finish eating her flapjack. Grandpa carried her upstairs and tucked her and Lily in. Then he said goodnight again before he gently closed the bedroom door.

The room was dark, but when Lily shut her eyes she could imagine the moonbeams and stars and the smiley moon outside. She thought Izzy was asleep until there was a sleepy whisper from next to her. "Night, night, Lily." Izzy yawned. "Thank you for being my big sister today."

"Night, night, Izzy," Lily replied. "Night, night, Piggy." Soon Izzy was giving little snores. Lily's eyes began to feel heavy too. "Goodnight Grandma and Grandpa and Hector and Jessie and Bessie," she said sleepily. "And night, night, magic jar," she whispered, just before she fell fast asleep.

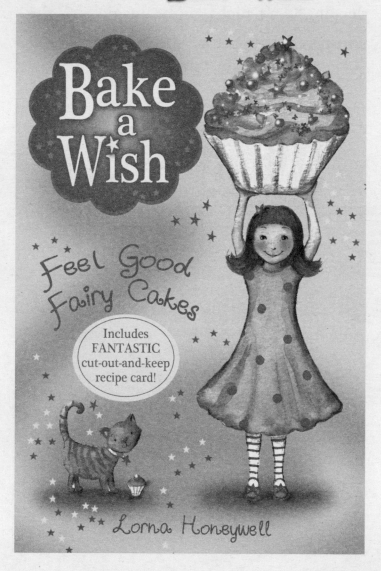

Bake a Wish

Get-Better Jelly

Includes FANTASTIC cut-out-and-keep recipe card!

Lorna Honeywell